Kugel For Hanukkah?

With love and gratitude to my family. —G.M.E.

For my nieces, Abi & Rose Hirsen. Happy Hanukkah! —R.A.

KAR-BEN PUBLISHING, INC.
A division of Lerner Publishing Group, Inc.
241 First Avenue North
Minneapolis, MN 55401 USA
1-800-4-KARBEN

Website address: www.karben.com

Main body text set in Billy Infant Regular 16/22
Typeface provided by SparkyType

Library of Congress Cataloging-in-Publication Data

The Cataloging-in-Publication Data for *Kugel for Hanukkah?* is on file
   at the Library of Congress.
978-1-5415-3464-3 (lib. bdg.)
978-1-5415-3471-1 (pbk.)
978-1-5415-6119-9 (eb pdf)

Manufactured in the United States of America
1-44881-35730-10/23/2018

Kugel For Hanukkah?

Gretchen M. Everin

illustrated by Rebecca Ashdown

KAR-BEN
PUBLISHING

When sunlight hid behind the trees and moonlight blew kisses to the snow, Hanukkah arrived.

I lit the shamash and the first candle.
Grandma said the blessing. Then we feasted on
crispy potato latkes with sweet applesauce.

When it was time to open presents, Grandma's gift was a jar of candied cranberries. I've really been hoping for a pet. Like a cuddly puppy . . .

But I got something very *un*-cuddly—a hard metal lamp.

The next night, I lit the shamash and *two* candles. Grandpa said the blessing. Then we munched on crispy carrot latkes with tangy sour cream.

When it was time to open presents, Grandma got a fancy kind of chocolate chips. Maybe I'd get a fancy feather-y parakeet?

The next night, I lit the shamash and *three* candles. Mommy said the blessing. Then we noshed on crispy turnip latkes with sweet brown sugar.

When it was time to open presents, Grandma got some spicy cinnamon sticks. Was I going to get a spunky little kitten?

No. I got a squeezy-squirty spray bottle.

What is going on here?

The next night, I lit the shamash and *four* candles. Daddy said the blessing. Then we enjoyed a dinner of crispy beet latkes with creamy yogurt.

When it was time to open presents, Grandma got a teeny tiny bottle of vanilla. I thought I might get a teeny tiny hamster!

Wrong again. I got a big branchy plant.

The next night, I lit the shamash and *five* candles. My big brother said the blessing. Then we nibbled on crispy parsnip latkes with cinnamon and sugar.

When it was time to open presents, Grandma got a shiny baking dish. Maybe I was getting a proud turtle with a shiny shell.

Nope. I got a shiny ceramic bowl.

The next night, I lit the shamash and *six* candles. My big sister said the blessing. Then we dined on crispy yam latkes with chunky applesauce.

When it was time to open presents, Grandma got a soft, ruffly apron. I was sure I'd get a soft, fluffy rabbit!

I did get something fluffy but it wasn't a rabbit.

It was a fluffy white sweatshirt.

The next night, I lit the shamash and *seven* candles. My grandpa said the blessing. Then we feasted on coconut latkes with yummy veggie salsa.

When it was time to open presents, Grandma got a thick heavy cookbook. Maybe I'd get a sturdy guinea pig!

But I got a thick, heavy book too!

The next night, I lit the shamash and all *eight* candles. I said the blessing. Then we enjoyed a dinner of everything-but-the-kitchen-sink latkes with sweet applesauce and tangy sour cream.

When it was time to open presents, Grandma got squishy, squashy oven mitts.

When it was my turn, there were no presents left!

I looked under the table.

I looked in the closet.

I looked behind the curtains.

But there was nothing for me.

Not even a goldfish.

How could there be no present for me? But
grandma put her arms around me and winked . . .

We went into the kitchen. One by one, she took out all her Hanukkah presents. Together we boiled and whisked and baked and *ding*! It was done.

My very favorite treat—kugel!

"Kugel for Hanukkah?" I asked.
"Why not?" said grandma.

Ding-dong! Someone was at the door.
"Better get that," said Grandma with a secret smile.
So I did. I loved my new iguana right away!

"What will you name her?" everyone wanted to know.

"Kugel," I said proudly.

"Her name is Kugel."

Cranberry Chocolate Chip Hanukkah Kugel

8 oz. egg noodles, uncooked
4 large eggs
⅓ c. granulated sugar
1 c. sour cream
1 c. cottage cheese, pureed in a blender or food processor

½ tsp. vanilla extract
½ tsp. ground cinnamon
⅓ c. chocolate chips
⅓ c. dried cranberries
2 Tbsp. butter

1. Ask an adult to help you make Hanukkah Kugel.

2. Preheat oven to 350 degrees.

3. Butter the inside of a large casserole dish or 9x9-inch pan.

4. In a large pot, boil egg noodles, according to package directions.

5. In the meantime, mix eggs, sugar, sour cream, cottage cheese, vanilla, cinnamon, chocolate chips, and cranberries in a medium bowl.

6. Drain egg noodles and add to the mixture. Stir until well combined.

7. Pour into casserole dish and bake for one hour or until the kugel pulls away from the sides of the dish and a knife inserted into the center comes out clean.

Makes 8-10 servings. Cover and refrigerate any uneaten kugel.